We Had a Picnic This Sunday Past

Jacqueline Woodson

ILLUSTRATED BY Diane Greenseid

We Had a Picnic

Hyperion Books for Children
New York

This Sunday Past

Printed in Singapore.
FIRST EDITION
1 3 5 7 9 10 8 6 4 2

Library of Congress Cataloging-in-Publication Data

Woodson, Jacqueline.
We had a picnic this Sunday past / by Jacqueline Woodson ;
illustrated by Diane Greenseid—1st ed.
p.   cm.
Summary: A young girl describes her various relatives and the
foods they bring to the annual family picnic.
ISBN 0-7868-0242-1 (trade)—ISBN 0-7868-2192-2 (lib. bdg.)
[1. Family life—Fiction. 2. Picnicking-Fiction. 3. Afro-Americans—
Fiction.] I. Greenseid, Diane, ill. II. Title.
PZ7.W868We   1997
[E]—dc20

96-16312

The artwork for each picture is prepared
using acrylic paint on paper.
The text for this book is set in 18-point Felt Tip.

For Kali, Sadie Rain, and Madeline Ivy
—J. W.

For Phyllis and the Hamilton High School Babies
—D. G.

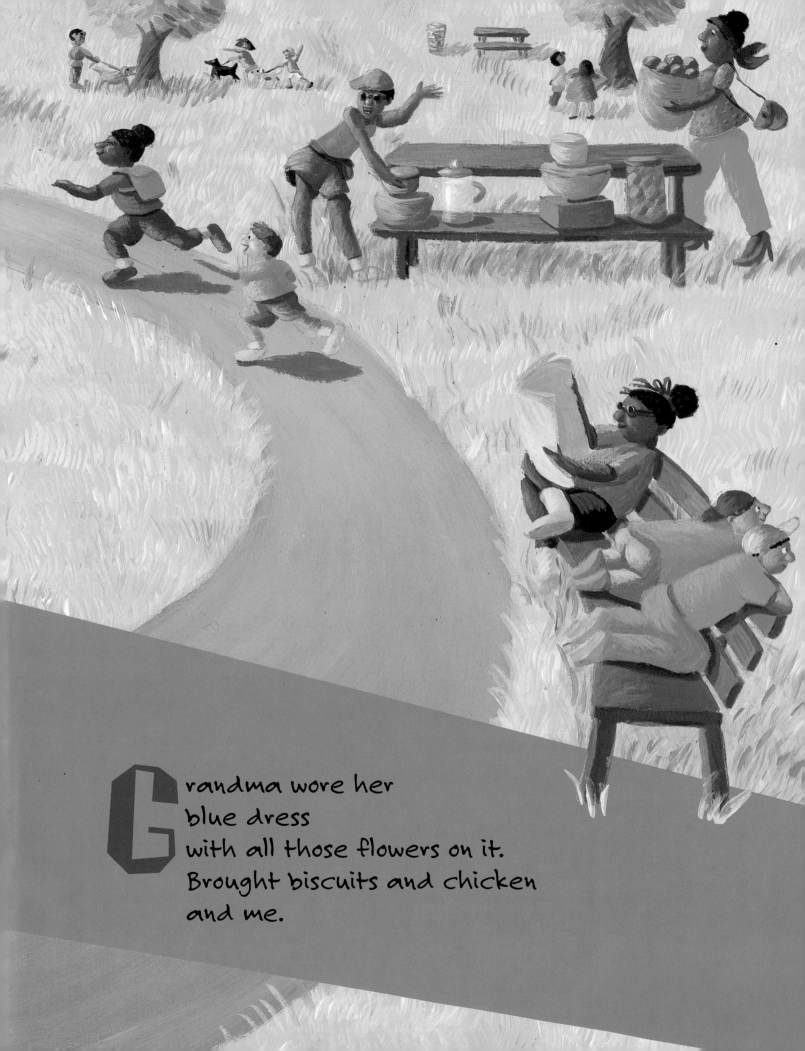

Grandma wore her
blue dress
with all those flowers on it.
Brought biscuits and chicken
and me.

Everything she made a big show of putting out. Got up at four this morning to make this chicken. Best batch I ever fried. These biscuits just as tasty. Can't chew for swallowing, can hardly swallow 'cause you'll be too busy reaching for more. And look at my grandchild. Just as pretty as a day. Turn and show them that dress I made you, Teeka.

Oh, how Grandma can brag when she wants to. Then turning to me she whispered,

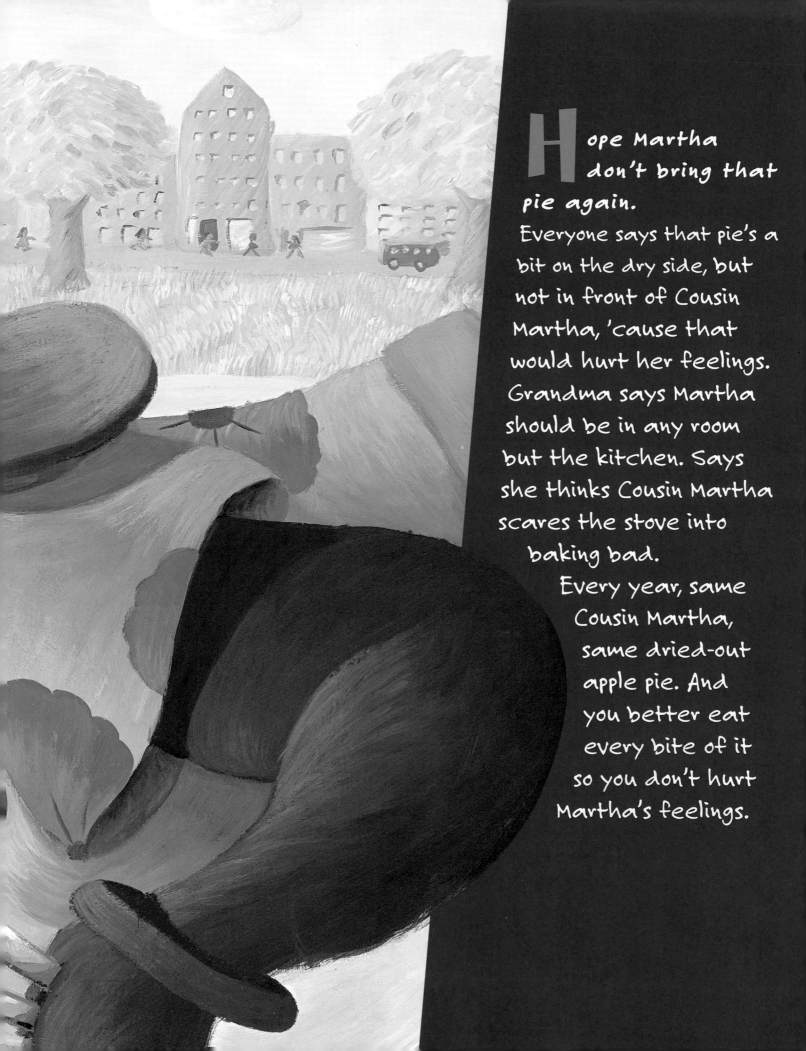

Hope Martha don't bring that pie again. Everyone says that pie's a bit on the dry side, but not in front of Cousin Martha, 'cause that would hurt her feelings. Grandma says Martha should be in any room but the kitchen. Says she thinks Cousin Martha scares the stove into baking bad.

Every year, same Cousin Martha, same dried-out apple pie. And you better eat every bite of it so you don't hurt Martha's feelings.

Luther is Grandma's oldest boy. He married Lucinda. Now they have Terrance, mean old cousin of mine. Terrance brought plastic flies, put them right on Auntie Sadie's sweet cob corn. Goodness, can my Auntie Sadie scream!

And give an ear a pinch if it needs one.

And whisper to Grandma, **You seen hide or hair of Martha's pie?**

ncle Luther
set a loaf of
cinnamon bread in the
center of things.
Grandma, smiling just as proud, said,
Can't my boy bake himself some bread!

Look at my second cousin Laurie's son, Jefferson.
He thinks he's so cute. **Hmph!**

Auntie Kim's my all-time favorite.
She's the smart one—teaches second
grade, I whispered to Paulette.
(Paulette's no relation—just my best friend.)
Don't go bragging, Grandma said, nudging
me. But you can tell she's just as proud.

Auntie Kim doesn't want to marry (and
maybe me and Paulette won't, either).
I brought some cranberry muffins,
Auntie Kim said, **and cookies
shaped like angels for my angel,**
handing one right
to me.

hen Cousin Trevor came—empty-handed.

Pretty-boy Trevor walking into that park with a handful of nothing.

Can't eat air, I whispered to Paulette.

Don't be a smartie, Grandma said, but you know she was thinking the same exact thing. Cousin Trevor picked daisies as he strutted up, talking about daisies for all the pretty ladies.

Humph, Grandma said, frowning.

Humph, me and Paulette echoed.

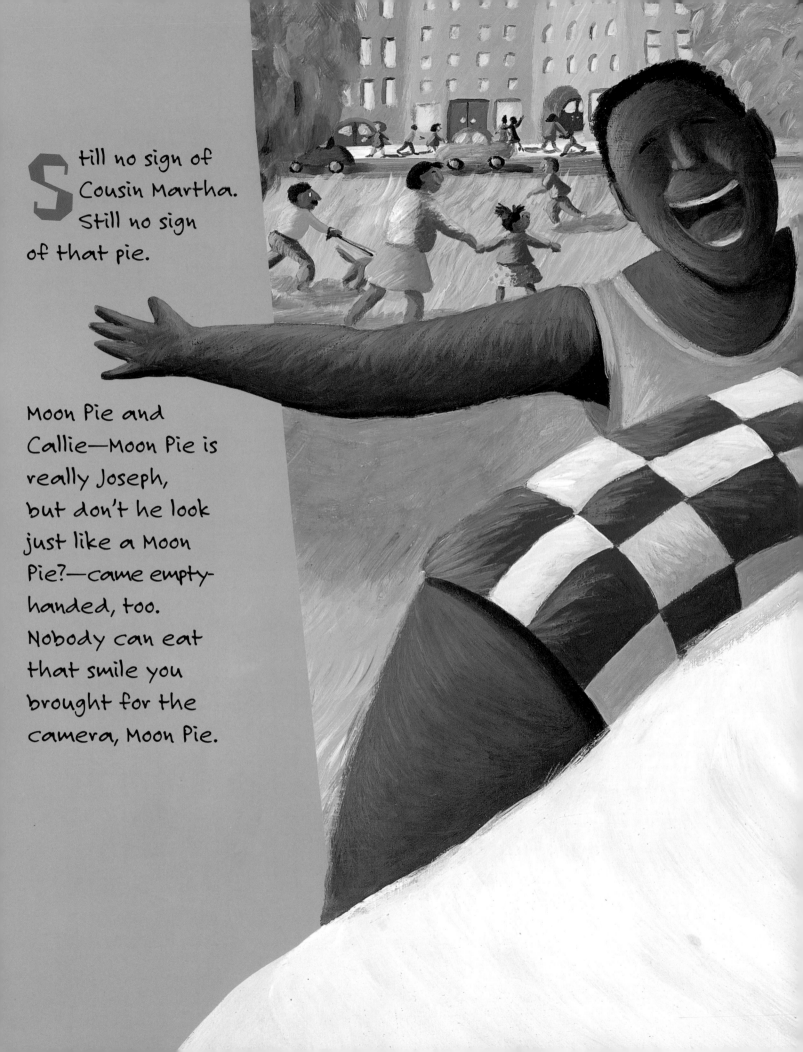

Still no sign of Cousin Martha. Still no sign of that pie.

Moon Pie and Callie—Moon Pie is really Joseph, but don't he look just like a Moon Pie?—came empty-handed, too. Nobody can eat that smile you brought for the camera, Moon Pie.

Sister Carol and Reverend Luke toted the Bible to the picnic. Reverend Luke can eat like the devil—strange, since he's such a holy man.

Little Astrid, two front teeth missing, trailed behind them carrying a pail of peaches fresh as summer.

Tooth fairy bring you anything? Paulette wanted to know. **Got a quarter for them,** Astrid said, and held out his hand to show us the shiny quarter there.

hen Mr. Pete came running—
he's got a thing for Grandma.
Mr. Pete, well, you can set
that sweet-potato pie right
over here by me, I said.

Wasn't that peach cobbler Miss
Mary's daughter Pat brought
just out of this world?

And yams and potato
salad and collards, a big
old ham, Grandma's
chicken fried crisp
and tender, melt-in-
your-mouth
cornbread . . .

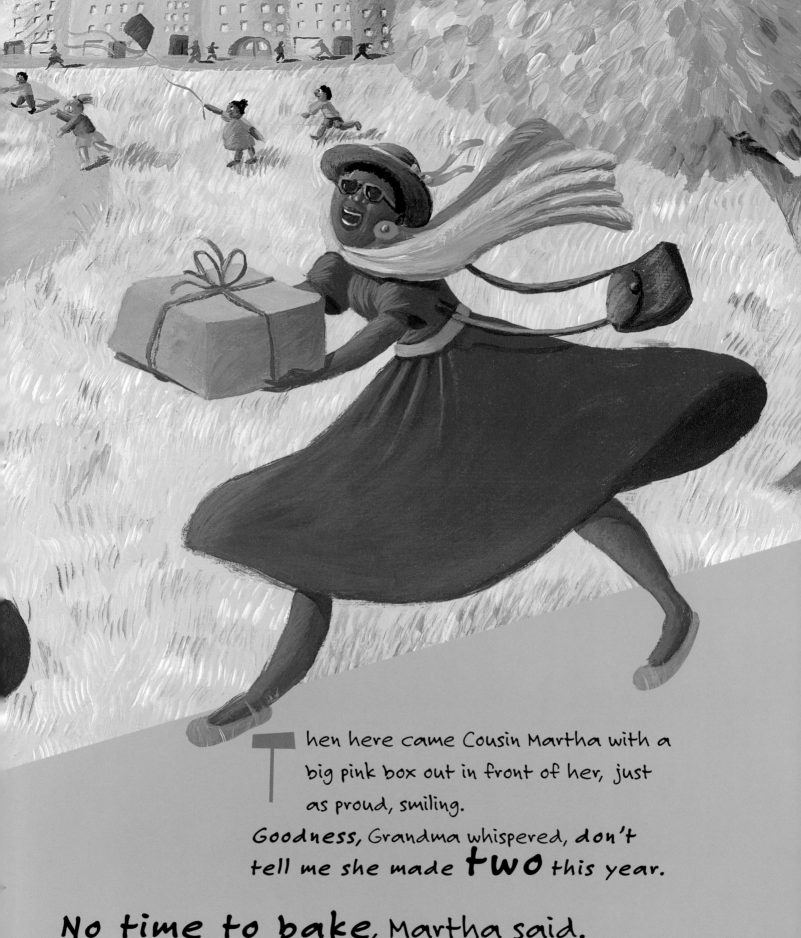

hen here came Cousin Martha with a big pink box out in front of her, just as proud, smiling.

Goodness, Grandma whispered, don't tell me she made **two** this year.

No time to bake, Martha said.

Store-bought cake and my apologies.

Oh, but Cousin Martha, Grandma said, all year long, I've been thinking about your pie.

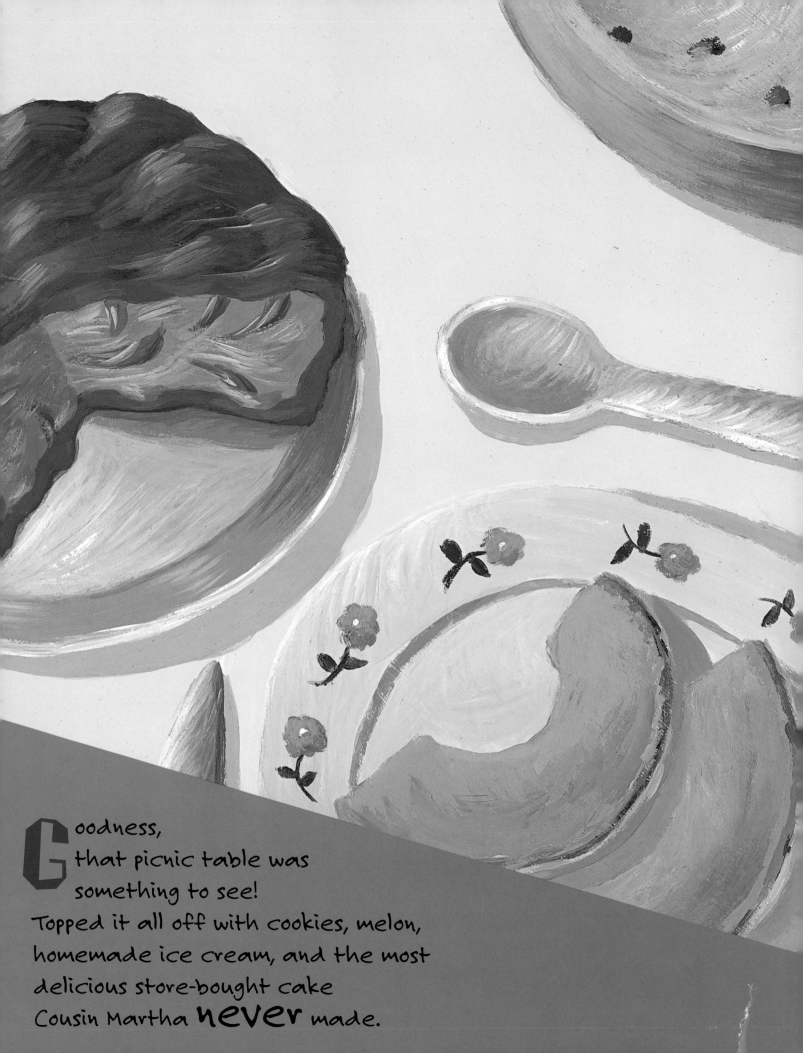

G oodness,
that picnic table was
something to see!
Topped it all off with cookies, melon,
homemade ice cream, and the most
delicious store-bought cake
Cousin Martha **never** made.

We had a picnic this Sunday past.

You should have been there.